I'M GOING TO GRAMMA'S IN MY PAJAMAS!

written by: Barbara Berg Mics — illustrated by: Tyler Ptaszkowski

Mama wakes me with a shout
Before the sun even comes out

She says, "Wake up, sleepyhead!"
But I just want to stay in bed...

I know just what to do...
I'm going to Gramma's in my pajamas!

GRAMMA'S
HOUSE
5 miles

③

Gramma will let me do whatever I please...
Even if I spend the whole day in my jammies!

Mama says I have to eat food that is good for me...

But all I want to eat is cookies, ice cream, and candy!

I know just what to do...
I'm going to Gramma's in my pajamas!

Gramma will never tell me no
Even if I want cookies, ice cream, and jell-o!

Mama says it's time to clean up and put away
But I just want to make a mess and play all day!

I know just what to do...
I'm going to Gramma's in my pajamas!

Gramma gets so happy when I walk through the door...

She will let me play with markers and color on the floor!

Thank you!

CHOMP!

(12)

Mama says it's time to take a bath...

13

But I don't want anything to do with that!

I know just what to do...
I'm going to Gramma's in my pajamas!

GRAMMA'S HOUSE

(15)

Gramma will say I'm clean as can be
There's never too much dirt on me!

GRAMMA'S
HOUSE

16

Mama says it's time to brush my teeth...

But I just want to eat cereal with my feet!

I know just what to do...
I'm going to Gramma's in my pajamas!

Gramma will say I can brush a little later
She says I have teeth like an alligator!

Mama says it's time to go to bed...
But I would rather watch a movie instead.

I know just what to do...
I'm going to Gramma's in my pajamas!

Gramma will let me stay up all night long
She will give me hugs and sing me a song

23

Mama says it's getting late
But I'm not sleepy yet, I'm feeling great!

I know just what to do!
I'm going to Gramma's in my pajamas...
AND I'M SLEEPING OVER!!!

98019245R00017

Made in the USA
Lexington, KY
03 September 2018